I0640708

William Henry Harrison

The Lazy Lays and Prose Imaginings

William Henry Harrison

The Lazy Lays and Prose Imaginings

ISBN/EAN: 9783337366483

Printed in Europe, USA, Canada, Australia, Japan

Cover: Foto ©Andreas Hilbeck / pixelio.de

More available books at **www.hansebooks.com**

THE

LAZY LAYS,

AND PROSE IMAGININGS.

WRITTEN, PRINTED, PUBLISHED, AND
REVIEWED BY

WILLIAM H. HARRISON.

A.D. 1877 (POPULAR CHRONOLOGY;)
A.M. 5877 (TORQUEMADA;) A.M. 50,800,077 (HUXLEY.)
38 GREAT RUSSELL STREET, LONDON.

CONTENTS.

SOME of these Poems and Prose Essays have
been previously printed in daily newspapers,
and in serial publications, whilst the others
are now issued for the first time. "*Wirbel-
bewegung*" was originally published in *The
Engineer*, and "How Hadji Al Shacabac was
Photographed" in *The British Journal of Pho-
tography*.

This first edition of some of the Author's
Collected Writings is now dedicated, without
permission, to the inhabitants of the United
Kingdom of Great Britain and Ireland, the
Islands in the British Seas, and the town of
Berwick-upon-Tweed; also to the rest of the
dwellers upon the Terrestrial Globe.

THE LAY

OF

THE LAZY AUTHOR.

———

On the softest of banks in the silent wood,
    All screened from the summer sky,
And the piercing rays of the noonday sun,
We'll lazily watch the streamlet run,
And the bright-eyed water-rats splashing in fun,
Free from all fears of a Cockney gun,
    Or the grave of a London pie.

And we'll dreamily watch the squirrel aloft,
    A-wagging his scrumptious tail,
Swinging amain on the slender birch
Right up in the clouds. What a dangerous perch!
If that twig should give a wind-driven lurch
He'll fall; and his partner in vain will search
    For his æronautical trail.

And we'll hear the buzz of the humble bee,
   As he plays his laziest tune;
Closing our eyes whilst his drowsy hum
Gently tickles the tympanum's drum,
And his poor little wings grow weary and numb,
Uplifting that body as big as a plum,
   On the hottest day in June.

And I'll write some verses for young and old,
   Mixed up with prose as well;
And when readers ask on this hottest of days,
What I mean by idly presenting as "lays"
Interspersed non-poetical prize es-says—
I'll murmur deep down in my drowsy maze,
   "It's really too warm to tell;

"Decide the question to suit yourselves,
   "And don't be misled by me;
"Just keep your thoughts as free as the wind:
"When a theory's crude you invariably find
"Some good-natured friend so awfully kind,
"As to try in advance to bias your mind;
   "*I* leave you perfectly free."

Yes, the mind shall wander in fancy free,
      Like waves on the rippling stream;
Comedy, tragedy, science, and fun,
In my lays shall find a place each one,
Like citron and sweets on a twopenny bun,
And shall vanish again when their *rôle* is done
      In my phantasmagorial dream.

Now, fare-thee-well, my listeners dear,
      After this passing peep,
At the lazy one who sings this lay,
On a woodland bank on a summer's day,
Whilst a fairy's eyes, in their gentle way,
On her most devoted loved one play,
      As he sinks in tranquil sleep.

On the cover of this book is a fine Griffin or "Gryphon," a time-honoured bird, who, in the days of old, kept guard over treasure, and protected it from appropriation by his natural enemies, the one-eyed Arimaspians of northern regions. The particular Arimaspians upon whom our Griffin is keeping watch, are those American publishers who may gaze upon this book with a single and undivided eye to their own personal interests. What they have to expect should they interfere with the Griffin and his trust, has thus been told by Milton:—

As when a gryphon, through the wilderness,
  With wingèd course ore hill or moarie dale,
Pursues the Arimaspian, who by stelth
  Had from his wakeful custody purloind
The guarded gold.
Paradise Lost. Book II.

THE LAY

OF

THE NEWSPAPER EDITOR.

A REVIEW OF "THE LAZY LAYS."

In a column of books on our table piled,
  We perceive *The Lazy Lays*,
And the work having been thus observed by Us,
  We feel it deserves great praise.

But Our space is so small in these stirring times,
  For aught but weighty themes,
And the Universe needs so much care from Us,
  That We shun all rhyming dreams.

Our greatly increased circulation just now,
  Drives tremors through Church and State,
But advertisements brought up to ten p.m.,
  Will not reach Our hands too late.

We regret the jealousy, envy, and hate
   Rival poets will show, and their fuss
At Our words for this book, but We say once more,
   That *The Lays* have been seen by Us.

       The Scilly Islands' " Trumpet Blast."

THE SONG

OF

THE PAWNBROKER.

———

[When the Vale of Neath Railway was extended to
Swansea, the Mayor and Corporation of that town invited
the Directors of the Swansea and Neath Railway Company to a public breakfast, on the morning of the opening
of the new line.   The following verses were written at
the time the public raised the question, whether the local
authorities were or were not justified in defraying the
expenses of the breakfast out of the rates.]

Oh, plesh my heart ! Oh, plesh my heart !

   Old Ikey's heart ish sad,

To see de vaste in monish made

   It drivsh me almost mad.

Four hundred poundsh ! Four hundred poundsh !

   In public breakfast shpent ;

All losht !—all down their gaping throatsh

   De lovely monish went.

Four hundred poundsh! Four hundred poundsh!
　　Mine heart ish breaking—oh !
'Twould buy a nish new Shynnygogue ;
　　A mountain of old clo'.

De leetle boys vat valks de street,
　　And pull my gaberdine,
Vould never vaste good monish so,
　　De shilds are moche too keen.

Let all de monish you don't want
　　Be to old Ikey shent,
And he will lend to Christian dogsh
　　At shixty-shix per shent.

Lisht to an uncle's kind advish,
　　And hear my gentle callsh,
Or I will leave your vasteful town,
　　And so will my three ballsh.

IKEY BEN SOLOMONS.

The Castle.

———

In the silence of eve when the shadows were falling,
    And the rocks and the twilight grew pallid and
        grey,
I gazed on a castle once famous in story,
    And thought upon those who had long passed
        away.

Round the ivy-clad turrets the sea-birds were
        screaming,
    And the torrents beneath in their murmuring
        flow,
Sighed a sorrowful dirge, 'mid the gloom and the
        darkness,
O'er the graves of the mighty ones sleeping
        below.

B

I gazed on the moat with its cold icy water,
  On the courtyard and terrace with nettles o'er-
    grown;
Through each dark winding passage my footsteps
    re-echoed,
  And I silently mused as I wandered alone.

The rack and the dungeon, the chain and the
    fetter,
  Have long done the work of oppression and
    wrong;
But their dark reign of terror has vanished for
    ever,
  For the truth has prevailed o'er the power of the
    strong.

Oh, beautiful ruin, a moral thou teachest:
  Thy dark desolation, thy dust and decay,
Are but emblems and types of tyrannical ages,
  Which are fading full fast, and must soon pass
    away.

I wish not to see thee again in thy splendour,
  Of pomp and magnificence—fleeting as sand—
O'er the race of humanity freedom is dawning,
  And a happier time for mankind is at hand.

Of the nations of earth the foundations are shak-
      ing,
  For purposes, deeper than mortal can tell,
Are working and weaving with men and their
      passions,
  And ruling the universe wisely and well.

THE LAY

OF

THE FAT MAN.

[Written shortly after the publication of Mr. Banting's
essay instructing stout people how to reduce their
size.]

How many a happy though indolent hour,
　Do we pass o'er the pages of Scott,
Till we seem to live in the days of old,
　And the present is all forgot.
For the air he peoples with life-like forms,
　And teems with fire his page,
As he leads by the power of his master mind
　Through the scenes of a bygone age.

But the pages of Banting are sweeter by far,
    'Tis nice o'er his writings to dwell;
His smiles for the lean, and his tears for the fat,
    Are kinder than mortal can tell;
The lean ones of earth he envelops in oil,
    And warms with an unctuous fleece,
Whilst the lubberly man, the two-leggèd globe,
    Is quickly distilled of his grease.

Yet I hate the old man who could sit down and write
    Such a volume on animal fat,
Who weighs himself every day in the scales,
    Exclusive of coat, boots, and hat;
So cover him o'er with oblivion's shroud,
    Then shelve him as fast as you can,
And we'll all of us drop a large marrow-fat tear
    O'er the grave of the greasy old man.

THE

POETRY OF SCIENCE.

———

O say not Science lacketh charms
   To woo the poet's pen,
To swell the pages of romance,
   Or thrill the souls of men ;
Her's is a realm of fairy land,
   A scene of endless change,
Where eye and ear are all confused
   With wonders passing strange.

She binds the eternal elements,
   She yokes them to the plough,
And iron steeds with hearts of fire
   Speed at her bidding now ;

Deep in the Ocean's solitude
  She her bright name engraves,
Unscathed she treads its golden sands
  And cleaves its surging waves.*

She joins the nations of the earth
  With mystic net-work bands,
Binding in common brotherhood
  The dwellers in all lands ;
Whilst through these wondrous arteries
  The lightning pulses thrill,
Bearing glad news of " Peace on Earth,"
  To all mankind, " Goodwill."

---

* "Bridges, unsupported by arches, can be made to span the foaming current ; man shall descend to the bottom of the ocean safely, breathing, and treading with firm steps on the golden sands, never brightened by the light of day. Call but the secret powers of Sol and Luna into action, and behold a single steersman sitting at the helm guiding the vessel, which divides the waves with greater rapidity than if she had been filled with a crew of mariners toiling at the oars. And the loaded chariot, no longer encumbered with panting steeds, darts on its course with relentless force and activity. Let the simple elements do their duty ; bind the eternal elements, and yoke them to the same plough."--*Friar Bacon's Prophecy.*

She bends their orbits, and the stars
 Speed on their track of light,
Sparkling afar in heaven's dark hall,
 Like glories in the night;
The planets feel her lion grasp
 As their bright paths they run,
And with relentless laws she guides
 The Chariot of the Sun.

The trees relate their fairy tales,
 The plants unfold their store
Of wisdom and design, and tell
 Truths never dreamt before.
The lightning plays around her feet
 And does her bidding well,
The very stones break forth in song,
 List to the tales they tell :—

They tell how chaos ruled—how earth
 Lay wrapped in death-like sleep,
How silence reigned in majesty,
 And darkness veiled the deep.

They tell how life uprose on earth,
　　How forests clothed the land,
And step by step reveal the work
　　Of HIS Almighty hand.

Calmly in silence and in gloom,
　　In caverns of the earth,
They teach vain man the nothingness
　　Of his ephemeral birth ;
Show him dread scenes of former life
　　Long to destruction hurled,
And on earth's pillars bid him read
　　The history of a world.

Behold another votary still—
　　The light her aid has given—
Light, whose bright beams of purity
　　Rushed angel-winged from heaven.
Then fair Aurora lit the north,
　　And shook her streaming bars,
Then earth awoke, awoke to life—
　　Then sang the morning stars.

Yet learn, Enchantress, thy domain
   A limit still must know;
Thus far, O Science, is thine own—
   Farther thou canst not go.
In Councils of Eternity
   HIS wondrous ways were planned—
Ways that elude thy piercing eye,
   Defy thine iron hand.

Remotest ages yet untold
   Shall own thy powerful sway,
Till man with all his noble works
   Shall pass from earth for aye.
For ever teach him Nature's laws,
   Unfold his Maker's will,
Guide him in paths of light and truth,
   And lead him upwards still.

HOW HADJI AL SHACABAC

WAS PHOTOGRAPHED.

———

THE original of the following letter is written in the choicest Arabic, of which I here present my readers with a translation. The letter is from Hadji Al Shacabac, a gentleman who visited London on business connected with a Turkish Loan, to Ali Mustapha Ben Buckram, chief of the College of Howling Dervishes, at Constantinople:—

Sweet, O Ali! are the moments thus snatched from the hurry of existence, when in the silence of night I take up my quill to hold sweet communion with the friend of my youth. No longer, alas! can we tread together the gardens of Istamboul, listening to the sweet notes of the nightingale, with its wings glistening in the silver rays of the silent moon, its melody changing with each zephyr which gracefully undulates the leaves of the lofty palampore.

Happy be thy days, O Ali!—serene and peaceful the hours of thy existence! Sweet, indeed, is the memory of friendship, grateful the remembrance of affection unto the soul of Al Shacabac, who now, far away from the wise utterances of thy learned lips, languishes like the love-sick bulbul when deprived of the company of the rose. Allah is great; so now with sable fluid, and the quill of a grey goose, I tell thee, O Ali, of my fearful adventure with the wizards of the crystal cages, in this vast city of the infidels. May the graves of their fathers be eternally defiled!

Here, O Ali, people take portraits, and, in fact, pursue all occupations with the visible assistance of the Evil One. They traverse rivers on the backs of dragons, and float through air suspended to eggs of fiends, whilst on land screaming demons of fire, with red and green eyes of light, fly with a thousand infidels at once through the bowels of the earth. The shrieks of these fire demons are horrible, rivalling the cries of those livid angels Monkir and Nakir, who, says our Holy Prophet, question every unbeliever directly he is laid in the grave, and beat him on the temples with an iron mace till he roars with anguish. Yes; in this awful place, O Ali, they hatch birds, and I am told babies, by steam; and the barbers in their shops force the heads of their customers against a revolving wheel to clear the mud out of their brains.

Thou hast heard of the wicked Magi, or Worshippers of Fire, whom our Holy Prophet kicked out from his vast dominions as he would unclean dogs. A remnant of these unbelieving curs exists here, within the walls of this Unholy City, and gains, it is said, immense sums by taking portraits by the aid of foul incantations. Allah bismillah! It is said the giaours bottle sunbeams for this unholy purpose, and that the powerful and malignant Genii, Klo Ryne and Sil Ver, are their chief abettors. The wizards, unlike those

of yore who haunted the dark caverns of the
earth, live in glass cages upon the housetops.

I longed for my portrait to send to thee, O Ali,
and the fourteen wives who mourn because of
my absence in the land of the stranger; yet my
infidel friend, Sammi Ben Jones, was long in over-
coming my scruples against visiting these wizards
in their crystal cages. However, by his advice I
walked along the street of Mi Lend, where many
wizards, for the sum of sixpence in infidel money,
exercise their unholy incantations.

It was a fine morning. I walked along with
the dignity remarkable to my family, dressed in
my best pink breeches, yellow coat, and scarlet
turban, wondering whether I should have to pass
through many difficulties before one of the wizards
would allow me to enter his domicile.

My doubts were soon at rest. I was forcibly
seized, O Ali, by six of the filthy emissaries of
these magicians, who caught hold of my flowing
robes, thrust gleaming squares of crystal beneath
my very nose, each pulling me with all his force,

and uttering curses in the barbarian tongue against the others who sought to force me into their masters' abode.

"Allah kerim!" I exclaimed in fainting accents, "these dogs will murder me, and my bones will whiten in the land of the stranger."

Suddenly a dragoman in blue came along the path, uttering the cabalistic word "Moovon," which I entered afterwards in my note-book. At the sound of it the miserably-clad giaours each slunk into the entrance of his employer's den, and contented himself with verbal adjurations.

I entered one abode which seemed less repulsive than the rest, and asked the imp at the door to admit me to the seer, his master.

He shouted up the stairs, "Ollo! Eerz anothergui!" which I was afterwards told by Sammi Ben Jones means, "Make ready, O master! The Wise and Noble Hadji comes!"

Having taken the fatal step into the dark archway, I must confess, O Ali, my frame shook with terror—my trembling knees refused their office.

To propitiate the evil Genii I took my shoes from off my feet at the entrance, and proceeded along the passage to a flight of stairs, where I prostrated myself, bowing three times towards Mecca. I found myself raised from behind with startling rapidity and pain, caused by the toe of the giaour, who, according to the infidel custom, lifted me to my feet in this manner by the sole strength of his accursed leg. The pain I feel to this day, and I fear it will never leave me till I bathe in the pond blessed by Our Holy Prophet, which is supplied by two pipes from Al Cawthar, one of the rivers of the Paradise of the True Believers.

With faltering steps I trod the ricketty stairs, and at last stood before the portal of the dread abode, on the panels of which were inscribed fearful cabalistic signs of mystic import, and in large red characters the words "John Smith," which, I believe, formed the name of the vile son of Jehanum himself.

The door opened. The figure of the dread

wizard, with a fiendish grin across his thin face,
stood before my awe-struck gaze.

Directly he saw me he opened his eyes and
roared, "Omosis!" Then he sank into a seat, his
sides shaking with idiotic laughter.

In words of thunder he shouted to me in the
infidel tongue—"Aintew akure?" at which I was
ready to sink through the floor with fright.

He motioned me to a seat in a chair with no
bottom to it, and told me to gaze my hardest at
a small picture nailed to the wall.

O Ali! how shall I describe that picture? In
our native land nothing but the eyes of our houris
are visible to the stranger, yet here the women
run about wild without any keepers, have even
their necks bare, and are supposed to possess
souls. But the one in this picture, O Ali, stood
in a barbarian theatre. She was dressed only in
gauze, and was spinning round on one leg like
your tame monkey Korac when in the height of
his antics.

"Allah akbar!" said I, "What can equal the

c

wickedness of these Christian dogs! May their fathers' graves be for ever defiled."

The wizard next fixed the back of my neck in an iron instrument, so that I could not turn away my gaze.

"Staffir Allah!" I cried in agony, "the anguish of the bowstring cannot equal this. I choke! I expire! Shades of my fathers! The wretched Shacabac will soon die with the throes of suffocation, and skate over the bridge Al Sirat into the Paradise of the True Believers!"

I thought my last hour was nigh, especially when I saw the magician hide his head in a black curtain, as though he wished not to witness my agonies.

He then retired to his secret den, O Ali, muttering accursed incantations, and came out with a small cabinet constructed of cedar, in which, no doubt, a wondrous talisman was concealed. He placed this in a kind of cannon covered with a pall of funeral black, and then he pointed this direful weapon at my head. My hair stood on

end, my eyes dilated with terror, my parched
tongue clave to the roof of my mouth. He un-
covered the opening of the cannon. I sprang up
with a shriek of terror, the iron instrument of
torture still clinging to my neck, and with outstretched arms implored Allah to forgive me for
entering the unhallowed den of the wizard of the
crystal cage. In this attitude did the Evil Genii
take my portrait.

The magician again retired to his den, where
I heard the sound of running water; then he
returned with a plate of crystal, and show-
ing it to me made signs of approval, uttering,
in a commendatory tone, the words, "Tharz
astunner!"

But, O Ali, the picture of thy friend was ugly
in the extreme. The aspect of abject fright was
upon my countenance; stars were represented
bursting above my head, a long-tailed comet
streamed from my nose, whilst my body was
spotted all over, yea, even like unto that of the
monkey Korac. No doubt the mighty power of

the sun had copied the evil planetary influences
which in that direful moment had threatened
me, but were at the time invisible to mortal
eye.

I carefully tied the crystal tablet in my turban,
handing sixpence to the wizard as I turned to
leave. The red-haired monster jumped between
me and the door, and in the vilest language demanded "fibob," or five shillings. In vain I
expostulated and offered another sixpence, making
double his usual fee. With dreadful curses the
infidel dog threw me on the floor, and pressing
a bottle of bitter liquid labelled " Fixing" to my
lips, said he would give me " Fissik" if I did not
"forkout fibob"—at least, so I understood him.

The fear of this horrid threat of Fissik, who
is doubtless some demon under his command,
made me pay the five shillings, after which I
descended the stairs saddened in spirit. The imp
at the door demanded a fee, upon which I called
him the son of a burnt father, and made him a
long speech in the Turkish tongue.

O Ali! Friend of my soul! The night wanes
apace. Even as I write the sun tinges with
crimson and gold the light clouds of the East.
The winds of heaven blow gently through my
open window, and I think of the time when I
journeyed with thee on the road to Ispahan at the
same silent hour. I like not the turmoil and
noise of the busy city, and long for the time
when we shall once more tread together the
bowers of Al Kibar, and I shall again hear
from thy learned lips the true doctrines of Islam.
My mind is much disturbed by the invisible stars
and comets which lurk around me, so on my
return we will lay my crystal portrait before our
wisest astrologers to learn what these mystic
signs portend.

Fare thee well, O Ali! Friend of my bosom!
Peace be unto thee and thine house! Mayest
thou live long in the land of our fathers; and,
when thou art called to Paradise, mayest thou
receive the richest fruits of the tree Juba, which
produces pomegranates, grapes, and dates of a

taste unknown to mortals! Fare thee well, O
Ali! and pray that thy friend may be protected
from evil planetary influences, as well as the
demon Fissik.

AL SHACABAC.

THE LAY

OF

THE BROAD-BRIMMED HAT.*

I LOVE it! I love it! my broad-brimmed hat,

With its surface so smooth, and its crown so flat;

And often my memory wanders away

To the thrice happy hours of my boyhood's young
day,

And I dream of the shop where I patiently sat,

While grandmother purchased my broad-brimmed
hat.

---

* These verses have been set to music by Mrs. Weldon
(of Tavistock House, Tavistock Square, London), who
trained the celebrated "Gounod" Choir.

When the maids at a picnic get caught in the rain,
It's shelter they seek, nor seek it in vain;
And they say, as the water pours off round the
  brim,
"Good gracious! how much we're indebted to
  him—
To the funny old man who owns this large tile,
With his 'Verily, yea!' and benevolent smile;
With his sober-cut coat, and its lining of grey.
Oh! aint he a darling?—aye, 'Verily, yea!'"

Through the streets of the town I impressively
  walk,
Of attraction the centre, of gossips the talk,
And the little boys shout, "What a regular flat
Is that funny old man in the broad-brimmed hat!"
With my gingham umbrella their jackets I clout,
And ask if their mothers are sure they are out;
But the young rogues have always their answer
  quite pat—
"Friend! where didst thou purchase thy broad
  beaver hat?"

When the sorrows of life set in like a flood,
And the nations are reeking with warfare and
  blood,
Its influence steals o'er my senses like rain—
Assuaging my anguish, relieving my pain.
Earth's troubles depart, its dramas grow dim,
As I sink into slumber beneath the broad brim;
And my dear little brother, as well as the cat,
Oft takes a night's rest in my broad-brimmed hat.

The rocks may be rent and the sea become dry,
And the moon disappear from its place in the sky;
The sun may grow dim—a mere dusky red ball—
The empires of earth may totter and fall;
The idle may grin, and the wicked may frown,
The lowly despise, and the lofty look down,
And small boys be saucy, and rude, and all that,
Yet I'll love thee! I'll love thee! my broad-
  brimmed hat!

ST. BRIDE'S BAY.

LOST in thought, oft I wander to scenes that are
    fading—
  To scenes where bright hope and high thoughts
    were entwined;
And often in silence fond memory lingers
  O'er moments with bright recollections en-
    shrined:

When all joyous I gazed on the haven's bright
    waters,
  As sunset bedecked them with glories untold,
When the cave and the headland, the cloud and
    the billow,
  Seemed robed in a mantle of crimson and
    gold—

When on Druidstone sands in frolicsome gladness,
    We chased the short hours in that glorious
        light,
Till the glare from the far Bishop's Lighthouse
        was streaming,
    And the pale stars above told the march of the
        night—

When the moon shed her beams on the slumber-
        ing waters,
    Which in purity mirrored her image beneath ;
When faintly the lights in the far hamlets glim-
        mered,
    And the winds murmured low o'er the brush-
        wood and heath—

When the surge of the waves by the caverns re-
        echoed,
    Emitted a moan all weird-like and high,
As the incoming waters in ripples were breaking,
    Or streamed o'er the rocks with a sorrowful
        sigh.

Ye are dear to me ever, ye wild scenes of beauty,
  For life with its changes was happier then,
Far away from the clamour and care of the city,
  The clang of the hammer and bustle of men.

THE LAY

OF

THE MARKET GARDENER:

A RYGHTE MOURNFULLE STORIE.

———

A SOBER man was William Jones,
 Who ne'er was known to laugh;
The undertaker tried in vain
 To get him on his staff.

Long at the market-gardening trade
 Had dismal William toiled,
And seen his fondest hopes decay,
 His undertakings foiled.

And now upon the tool-house steps,
    Like a young Cushat dove,
He sat and sang the dismal tale
    Of unrequited love.

" My mind in early youth was choked
    With tares and poppies grim ;
'Twas disappointment sowed the seeds,
    And misery raked them in.

" Yes, sorrows rose to kill my joys,
    Like mushrooms in a night ;
The sunflower of my life is gone,
    My heart's-case has the blight.

" I fondly loved sweet Susan Gibbs,
    A solemn lass, and sad ;
She wept so much that people thought
    Her melancholy mad.

" As soon as I discerned her worth,
    In melancholy tones
I urged my love with sobs and sighs,
    And she replied with groans.

" While thus adown life's tearful scene
   So swimmingly we sailed,
A tailor from a neighbouring town,
   My mourning suit curtailed.

" Ah! false and fair is Susan Gibbs,
   She lately has began
To cut the tendrils of my heart—
   She loves the tailor man."

Now at the Plough and Harrow's tap
   Jones daily drank and pined,
So much her faithlessness did plough
   And harrow up his mind.

Said he—" My love to you was like
   The needle to the Pole,
Yet breaches come, and now you sew
   Great stitches in my soul.

" Oh, cruel, cruel Susan Gibbs!
   With these sharp garden shears
I'll cut my thread of life in two,
   And quit this vale of tears."

"Oh William, don't! oh Billy, don't!
I'll constant prove and true."
"What care I for your 'Billy don't,'
Give me that *billet doux*."

With fearful looks he read the scrawl;
Susan recoiled with dread;
They both sheered off the cellar stairs,
And he sheared off his head.

Moral.

Now faithless lovers, warning take
From William Jones's fate;
Like Susan you may live to mourn,
But mourn, alas, too late.

Remember jealousy has eyes
As sharp as any fox,
And turned poor Jones's little trunk
Into a six-feet box.

"FAST FALLS THE EVENTIDE."

WHEN the setting sun in splendour
  Slowly sinks from mortal sight,
Crowns the earth with clouds of crimson,
  Robes the sea in living light—

When the rainbow hues of sunset
  Fading from the hills are seen,
And the night, with dusky mantle,
  Reigns our sable-shrouded queen,

Calming earth with all its passions—
  Envy, hatred, fear, and love—-
And the pale white stars are throbbing,
  Throbbing in the heavens above—

D

When earth's sister orb, ascending,
　　Tints with light each hillock green,
And the ferns, with dewdrops bending,
　　Glisten in the silvery sheen,

Then I feel how sin and sorrow
　　Stain the earth by mortals trod.
Far from man the troubled spirit
　　Seeks its fellowship with God.

OUR RAVEN.

He was a malicious bird, and in him all the evil propensities of his tribe appeared to be centred; he seemed to be continually meditating mischief, and there was roguery in every look. He had been in our possession some days before we christened him, there being a difficulty in finding a name bad enough to suit his deserts; but one morning as we were considering the subject, and the advisability of calling him "Beelzebub," he was observed to listen with marked attention, with his head on one side, and a diabolical sparkle in his eye; at last, to the surprise of all present, he pronounced, in a deep, hoarse voice, the name "Roger." Where he learnt it was never satisfactorily ascertained, but Roger became his name from that hour to the day of his death.

The maid-servants stood in bodily fear of him, and he knew it full well. Like most of his tribe, he was perfectly happy while trying the strength of his iron bill upon their ankles. He would also walk off with scraps of meat and mutton chops from before their eyes with the utmost gravity, knowing that they were afraid to molest him. On occasions of this kind there would be loud cries for " Bill," young buttons, who alone could manage the formidable Roger. The bird would pay little attention to their cries, till he heard the footsteps of Bill in the passage, when he would suddenly lose all his magisterial dignity, and run and drop the stolen dainty before the nose of the sleeping and innocent cat, after which he would jump on the table and shriek " Bill!" with the loudest of them.

Even in the coldest weather he thoroughly washed himself twice-a-day, till his beautifully glossy feathers shone again. After each bath, he usually mounted a sunny corner of the outhouse, and had a long talk to himself; here and there the words "Roger," "Bill," and "Hulloa," could be clearly distinguished, but the greater part of his recitation was unmeaning gabble.

When hungry he would shout "Bill!" at the top of his voice, till the red-haired individual in question made his appearance; then in a deep, solemn voice he would say "Roger," thereby intimating that, upon whatever important avocation his young friend might at that moment be engaged, it was imperative that Roger's wants should have immediate attention.

Every evening his eyes might be seen in the darkness, glaring down from the top of the kitchen cupboard, like those of an evil spirit, as he sat meditating dark and evil deeds for the morrow, like the raven of Barnaby Rudge.

Science was not neglected by him; he was an enthusiastic floriculturist. If a flower took his fancy, he would pull it up by the roots, carry it to another part of the garden, make a hole in the mould with his beak, and replant it. This would not have mattered much, but sometimes with the insane desire, perhaps, of forming a bouquet for some lady raven of his acquaintance, he would pluck the flowers, and not being able to bind the stalks together, would strew them over the pathway. Conchology also had its share of attention; for if a snail came in his way, he would divest it of its shell in the twinkling of an eye, and its unfortunate occupant would be gliding down Roger's throat before he could rightly tell what was the matter.

Through Roger I nearly lost the friendship of a young doctor, whom I had known ever since his christening. The doctor lived next door, and was partial to grapes—in fact, he prided himself upon his skill in growing them, and spent most of his leisure time in attending to a large vine at the back of the house. Early one fine morning Roger amused himself by nipping off the bunches one by one, and watching them fall on the ground below. The doctor saw the havoc that had been made, and was heaping maledictions upon the head of the depredator or depredators unknown, when a loud

"Hulloa!" caused him to look up, and Roger let fall the last bunch on his nose.

For this freak he was given away to a gentleman living half a mile off; but a few days afterwards he came tumbling in at the door in an apparently tipsy state, exclaiming, "Hulloa! Roger! hu-l-l-o-a!"

It was a dark, wintry night when a tremendous crash and a cry of thieves, alarmed the whole house, and going to the window which overlooked the garden, I saw a large dark hole in the red-tiled roof of one of the outbuildings, through which the rascals doubtless expected to force an entry into the house. Bill opened the garden door, and cautiously climbed up to the hole in the outhouse roof, when out popped Roger's head with a loud "Hulloa!" which so frightened the boy, he lost his hold, and slid off the roof to the ground.

Roger was whipped for that night's work, yet he amused himself next day by repeating the experiment. It was wonderful how he was able to move so heavy a body as a pantile, yet he did it, and as the outhouse stood a fair chance of being unroofed by his pranks, he was sent away a long distance into the country.

Like most mischievous people, he suffered for his tricks in the end. A ploughman was late one evening walking along the road near Roger's abode, and the raven began hopping and flying after him, shouting "Hulloa! Bill!" Now, Bill happened to be the name of the individual in question, so he fled from the apparition in terror, with the demoniacal bird speeding at his heels, his dark proportions much increased in size, through the dim light of the dusk of the evening. The man, who firmly believed that a fiend was pursuing him, at last could run no longer, so turned round and frantically beat poor Roger to death with a thick stick. He then carried the body back in triumph to the village, looking upon his achievement as a praiseworthy act rather than otherwise.

MATERIALISTIC RELIGION.

MATERIALISM is flourishing at the present day,
upsetting popular ideas by antiquity established,
and reducing everything to mechanics and mathe-
matics. Besides, it is about to put itself to the
test of experiment. Who has not heard of the
furnaces, the great anvil, and the steam-hammer,
about to be fitted up near Burlington House by
the chief philosophers of the day, to forge a new
religion by the proper manipulation of the right
chemical substances? Indeed, the only difficulty
is how to "hitch on" the mechanical religion
to human consciousness and aspirations; but the
temporary absence of this trifling link need be
no bar to the authoritative promulgation of the
doctrine of "the present orphanage of man, and
his future nonentity," or to the condemnation of

those opposed to it to the limbo of the unintel-
lectual.

Let us see what the scientific world knows
about the "matter" which we are to fall down
and worship. Until philosophers define what
they mean by "matter," all arguments based upon
a word to which several meanings are attached,
are necessarily not clearly stated.

The prevalent idea among physicists is, that
matter consists of a vast number of almost infinitely small atoms in a state of incessant vibration.
That these hypothetical atoms move is certain,
because material bodies change their volume
with every change of temperature. Make an
iron poker hot, and it is longer than it was when
cold. Hence, as the atoms in the extreme ends
of a hot poker are *measurably* farther from each
other than they were when it was cold, it is certain that they must have moved. It is supposed
that each little atom vibrates to and fro, and that
this vibration is what men call "heat." The
greater the atomic vibration, the hotter is the

substance, because the little atoms knock against the ends of the nerves in the hand with greater force, and the substance consequently feels warmer. If the temperature be lowered, the atoms swing over less space than before, consequently the poker contracts. If a sufficiency of heat be applied to the substance, the atoms swing so far apart that the force of cohesion is partially overcome, and the atoms roll over each other like so many marbles in a moving box. In this condition the substance is said to be "melted:" it is in the liquid state. Increase the heat, and the little atoms are so liberated that they fly to and fro, knocking against the sides of the vessel containing them. This is known as the gaseous state of matter.

The above hypothetical view of the nature of material bodies explains a vast number of physical facts, and is of great value in successful experimental physical research. It is the view held by most of the leading physical philosophers of the day.

Those objectors who deny that solid substances consist of particles in a state of incessant motion, are at variance with the best men in the philosophical world, and hold exceptional views about practical experiments connected with the expansion and contraction of solids. If, however, the hypothesis be admitted, then it is clear that to define what matter is, the materialist must define the nature of the little vibrating atoms.

In fact, the whole question—"What is matter?" rests upon the question—"What is an elementary atom?"

Nobody has ever seen one of them. They are infinitely beyond the reach of the most powerful microscope, since millions upon millions of them are required to occupy the space of a single cubic inch. There is the greatest difference of opinion in the philosophical world as to the ultimate constitution of atoms, and herein lies the justification of my assertion, that the argument for materialism is based upon a word having a vague, uncertain meaning.

Professor Tyndall thinks that, possibly, atoms are infinitely rigid little particles, something like minute bullets. Will he please explain how they build themselves up into living intelligent beings? If they do not so build themselves up, but flow to different positions around something invisible, what is that invisible something, and does it live when unclothed by matter?

Professor Sir William Thomson once promulgated the speculation, that atoms possibly consist of portions of an infinitely elastic fluid, thrown into a state of vortex motion; and Helmholtz has mathematically demonstrated that such motion, once set up, would continue to all eternity. By an "infinitely elastic fluid," is meant one destitute of viscosity, or fluid-friction—a fluid very similar in its nature to the interstellar ether.* If mate-

---

* A clever experiment, designed by Sir Wm. Thomson and Professor Tait, to show the great permanency of fluid vortex rings, even when a fluid not destitute of friction is used, was once exhibited by the latter philosopher at Edinburgh University. A large square wooden box had one of its ends taken off, and a piece of thick cloth was tied over this end. In the opposite end of the box was a round hole,

rialists believe solid substances to consist of vortex
rings, will they explain how the said rings build
themselves up into intelligent beings?

Not a few philosophers think that atoms consist of forces emanating from points, and points
have neither length nor breadth. Is this the
materialistic opinion? If so, it assumes that
there is no such thing as common matter at all,
in the sense in which the word is ordinarily
used.

Professor Huxley is inclined to think, with
Bishop Berkeley, that our knowledge of the

---

the size of a cheese-plate. The necks of two retorts entered one of the sides of the box; the one retort was made
to discharge hydrochloric acid gas into the box, whilst the
other supplied ammoniacal gas. When these two gases
mixed, white fumes were formed; consequently, the box
was continuously charged with dense white smoke. Every
time the cloth at one end of the box was struck by the
hand, a vortex ring of common air was forced out of the
round hole opposite; the said ring of air was made visible to
the eye by the white smoke it held in suspension. These
white rings floated about in the room for some little time
before their viscosity caused them to break up. Whenever two of these smoke-rings struck each other as they
floated about, they rebounded from each other as two indiarubber belts would have done.

external world depends on the nature of our sensations, and the way in which those sensations act
upon our consciousness. He says that if he were
compelled to choose between pure idealism and
pure materialism, he should select the former.

As it is a fact that the best philosophers of the
day do not know what matter is, and are divided
in opinion as to its nature, there is just cause
for complaint, that anybody should use the word
" matter " in the fundamental part of an argument
against any religious ideas which exercise a bene-
ficial moral influence upon society. There are
people who think that there is no such thing as
common matter, and that the external world is
the result of mental conditions governed by law.

THE LAY

OF THE

PHOTOGRAPHER.

A SCIENTIFIC BALLAD.

[IN the following poem the various manipulations incidental to the preparation of what are known to photographers as "dry plates," are allegorically described. Dry plates are much used in the photographing of landscapes.]

The American Origin of Pyroxyline.

Young Pyroxyline has come out of the west,

Where he lived with dark niggers, not very much

dressed.

All regardless of safety he plunged in the brine,

To keep watch and ward o'er the fair Iodine.

Bright, bright was his armour and gleaming his
    face,

The Meeting of Pyroxyline and Iodine.

As he seized his fair prize with a loving em-
    brace.

"Oh, Roxy! Ha, dun now! You've broken my
    fan!

I'll tell papa Tyndall, you naughty young man!"

The truth must come out, though it grieves me full
    sore,

Iodine cuts off the luminous rays, but allows the ultra-red to pass.

She for Tyndall, her parent, told fibs at the
    door;

To the ultra-red rays she said—"Come in and
    roam!"

But to those with bright colours said—"Pa's not
    at home!"

This demoralised maid, thus trained in deceit,

Iodine enters into union with Silver.

A rich store of silver resolved to escheat.

"I like not old Nitre," she sulkily said,

"But his silver galore—it is that I will wed."

E

Iodide of Silver causes Pyroxyline to turn yellow.

Poor Pyroxyline turned yellow with rage,
To see them united at that early stage.*
His spirits departed, he grew pale and thin,
Till the dear little man became nothing but skin.

The Nitric Acid is driven off, and the Iodide of Silver is dried.

And acid old Nitre soon gave up the ghost,
(Which was hunted by Crookes from pillar to post.)
And Iodine's heart, by a power from on high,
Like Pharoah's of old, was made rigid and dry.

The Pyrogallic developer separates some of the Iodine from the Silver.

Then a demon named Pyro invaded her home,
And exclaimed—"As my slave from this day you must roam."
"Oh! never!" she shouted, but ere she could wink,
He swept her away down oblivion's sink.

Astonishment of Philosophers.

* Indeed, Mr. Cottrell thought he had got her all,—
Her union with Nitre was quite a surprise;
E'en the great Mr. Spottiswoode said it was not as good
A match as she might have made, had she been wise.

A theoretical explanation.

A Woman's Rights preacher exclaimed, "The bold creature
Is a perfectly shameless and brazen-faced jade;
But you know for an F.R.S. no woman ever hesitates at the matrimonial grade!"

All her ill-gotten gains, which were stored in a *The separated Silver is of a black colour.*
    sack,

'Neath the glance of the fiend turned ashy and
    black.

" Aha!" said the demon, with caper and grin—

" Dead sea fruit always falls as the wages of
    sin."*

People shudder whenever they speak of the dead, *Bromine now supplants Iodine in dry-plate processes.*

And Bromine, her sister, now reigns in her stead,

And in elegant mourning may often be seen,

With the nearest relations of Pyroxyline.

When a baby photographer lies at the breast, *Photographers now abhor Iodine.*

In innocence peacefully taking its rest,

If you whisper false Iodine's name in its ear,

It awakes with a shriek, and turns pallid with
    fear.

---

  * Said one J. T. Indle,—" Crimes always enkindle *Evil acts bring their own retribution.*
     A lingering train of deception and woe ;
    Though you may try an' hide, be sure that Cyanide
    Will ever complete the fell work of Py-ro!"

The negative
film when dried
becomes rigid.

The darkness of night settled over the scene,

But sleepless and restless was Pyroxyline;

His hopes foully crushed, his happiness fled,

They found him next morning all stiffened and dead.

Appearance
of the poor
relations of
Pyroxyline.

The deceased's poor relations appeared on the scene:

First came Stewart, with a glass, to see things
    unseen;

Then Clifford came reading, with serious face,

His essay on sixteen dimensions in space.

More poor
relations.

And Simpson and Taylor appeared hand in hand,

Leading spirits are they in photographic's band;

Under the greenwood they sat themselves down,

And drowned all their sorrows in ale from the
    Crown.

News of the
death produces
grief.

To Huxley, and Lockyer, and Roscoe, and Stokes,

Clerk Maxwell fired off some molecular jokes,

But the news of the death caused a change in
    their air,

And they came to the funeral pale with despair.

Next came Serjeant Cox with Colonel Lane   A requiem is
prepared.
   Fox,
Also Vincent and White, with a ballotting
   box;
Soon Thomson spun in on a fine vortex ring,
And Crookes brought a requiem signed " Katie
   King."

All hushed was their chatter; a feeling of dread   The Funeral.
Crept o'er them upon the approach of the dead,
Borne by Odling and Caithness, and two or three
   more,
Who placed the remains on the sepulchre's floor.

Then a requiem was sung, and a few tears were   *Requiescat in*
pace.
   shed,
And an epitaph placed at the feet of the dead.
May philosophers all keep his memory green,
And pray for the soul of poor Pyroxyline.

HOW TO DOUBLE

THE UTILITY OF

THE PRINTING PRESS.

———

THE question of the more rapid and cheap dissemination of knowledge is one of interest to all who desire the promotion of the civilisation of the race, and a great step in the right direction may be made, by doing away with the enormous waste of space and paper in newspapers and books, caused by the unwise shape of the letters of the present alphabet. The letters at present in use were arbitrarily designed by the Phœnicians in primitive times, and roughly represented objects common about farms. The letter A was originally a rough representation of the head of a cow as shown in the first figure in the accompanying 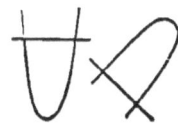 cut; in process of time the cow's head was turned round and made to point to heaven, as shown in the second figure, that position being afterwards discovered to be the most convenient. Ever since it was so placed, no further attempts have been made to economise space, nor can there be until the daily newspapers unite to gradually introduce letters of better form.

Why should we, to this day, be slaves to designs which probably originated with a prehistoric farm servant, who invented them to record his milk scores on the crown of his hat?

Why should the letter "W" be entitled to a shape which takes up so much more space than the letter "I"? A straight stroke, with a projection on one side only, will take up no more space than the letter "I" with its projections on two sides. In the following cut, and in the first group, each of the six new letters has projections on one

side only. By altering the shape of the projections, as shown in each letter of the next group,
other letters may be formed, and these again may

be multiplied by varying as before the position
of each projection; and further varieties may be
produced by the use of thin as well as thick
strokes, as shown in the last group. Thus it
is plain that some hundreds of letters may be
designed, each of which shall occupy no more
space than the letter "I." To show the economy
which would result, here are two lines, the one
composed of "I's" and the other of "W's":—

IIIIIIIIIIIIIIIIIIIIIIIIIIIIIIIIIIIIIIIIIIIIIIIIIIIIIIIIII
WWWWWWWWWWWWWWWWWWWWWWW

There are 56 "I's" in the preceding lines, and
23 "W's," or 2½ times as many of the former as
of the latter.* Considering then that no letter need

---

* Unless the information had been given, the reader
would scarcely have recognised the letter "I" in the long

occupy more space than "I" it is evident that an
enormous economy is possible, and that thousands
of tons of paper are wasted in this country every
year, to afford room for letters of irrational shape.
The daily newspapers alone can bring about a slow
reform in this matter, and the civilisation of the
world is considerably retarded until their managers
act upon the principles herein set forth, although
that action they must of necessity take sooner or
later.

How can the proposed improvement in the
shapes of letters be brought about in a practically
efficient way? If any small efforts were made by
one or two individuals, they would fail, and their
peculiar books would be laughed at by the un-
thinking multitude.   But five or six London daily
newspaper proprietors, after satisfying themselves

---

row of them printed above the row of W's. As another
example of the way in which the position of a letter may
affect its appearance, it may be mentioned that although
the upper and lower portions of the letter "S" are usually
supposed to be of the same shape and size, the lower half
is largest, as may be plainly seen when the letter is printed
bottom upwards, thus—"S."

of the utility of the idea, and the fact that its fulfilment would enable them to get twice as many advertisements as at present into one column, could bring it about without much trouble.   First, they would have to explain to their readers the value of the plan to society and to the progress of civilisation, and afterwards they would have to announce that once every three months they would alter the shape of one of the letters of the alphabet used in their journals.   They might begin with the frequently used letter M, and alter it to a shape which occupied no more space than the letter I. For the first three or four days the readers would feel worried by the change, but in a fortnight they would no more dream of going back to the old M than to the use of sedan chairs.   Then the journals must wait for three months, for if the public hate anything, it is personal improvement and instruction; so it would not do to move too fast. At the end of three months they might pluck up heart of grace and introduce another new letter. Each change would enable them to gain, say half-a-column of space in a daily paper. I do not see how any other persons than daily newspaper proprietors could hope to successfully make the proposed change; but the said proprietors could do it with the utmost ease. Printers, compositors, and type-founders ought to like the change, because the demand for printing is now greatly limited by the expense; and, as every editor knows, shoals of essays are at present, perhaps at no great disad vantage to the public, condemned to remain in manuscript, because of the cost of printing. The proposed slow alterations in the shapes of letters would give a great impetus to the printing trade.

After the shape of letters has been improved, the phonetic principle will have to be adopted, and long ages hence, when the public are educated up to the point, a new and shorter language will have to be invented. Why should any word be more than one or two syllables in length, thereby wasting time and money in speaking, writing, and printing? At present, men can speak faster than their listeners can think, but as the race grows more

nervous and more sensitive, the receptive powers
of the mind will be quickened, so that the advan-
tage of the abolition of all arbitrary language in
making oral communications will be greater than
at this day.

THE LAY

OF

THE MOTHER-IN-LAW.

———

A POOR weeping woman your sympathy asks,
   In her hour of affliction and grief,
When memory's pangs have set in like a flood,
   And she looks round in vain for relief.

Three daughters I had, fair as roses in June,
   But ingratitude reigns in them now;
For their poor troubled mother they care not a rap,
   And I'll tell you the why and the how.

My eldest girl, Edith, had suitors by scores,
   But I told her with feelings of pride,
How her Pa in the city was "Monarch of all
   He surveyed" on the Lombard Street side.

So lovers and schemers of every kind,
    Good and bad, old and young, false and true,
Were quickly deputed to Coventry's shade,
    And I think she showed wisdom—don't you?

Oh, I fed her true pride as a mother should do,
    Till she frequently used to aver,
Come weal or come woe she'd have none but a
        prince—
    But no prince volunteered to have her.

Now she's old, and bad-tempered, and shrivelled,
        and wan,
    And asserts that I blighted her youth—
Says I taught her to sacrifice nature to pride,
    And to substitute scheming for truth.

She says I encouraged an indolent life—
    A life useless to God and to man,—
That she wishes the grave had closed over her
        head
    Ere I steeped her in plotting and sham.

Pretty language, I'm sure, for a mother to hear!
  I beg pardon, sir; what did you say?
Then I am not a mother-in-law after all?
  Not so fast with your guessing, I pray.

Now Ethel, her sister, the gentlest of girls,
  Fell in love with a man near Tor Bay,—
A lawyer whose conscience, forsooth, kept him
      poor!
  So I soon got him out of the way.

With manners most cool and civility scant,
  I froze all his approaches to me;
And Ethel I lectured severely, and said
  That her conduct was shocking to see.

So that little matter I nipped in the bud,
  But it cost her full many a tear;
And often the heart-broken look of the child
  Distressed me with undefined fear.

Like the rest of my class I "went in" for a
    lord,
  But found most of them civil and cool,
Till I caught a *roué* by his friends cast away
  As a ne'er-do-well scapegrace and fool.

Now to tell you the truth I did not like this
    match;
  I was troubled with horrible dreams;
But for theories based on religion and truth,
  Should I give up my business schemes?

No. I did it. The child was too young to resist,
  And I rose in position and pride;
She said, and said truly, I ought to know best,
  And her tears I consolingly dried.

We cleared off the mortgages, "did up" the park;
  Oh, the envy of thousands were we!
The lacqueys were humble, the gamekeepers meek,
  And the parson most civil to me.

Though splendour and luxury reigned at the
    Hall,
  Foul fiends ran riot in our hearts;
A home without love, formed to serve as a
    show,
  Could not shield us from conscience's darts.

The details, my friends, it is needless to tell,
  You can see them on every side;
I stand not alone in impaling young lives
  On the spears of show, title, and pride.

'Tis a terrible thing the affections to crush—
  To fetter with permanent gyves;
I would I had known the effects in a home,
  Of my traffic in human lives.

First came anger, then cruelty, hate, and neglect,
  And I wished that my work were undone;
They now live apart—God asunder has put
  Those whom I had conjoined into one.

F

In buying and selling I feel quite at case,
   And must I sell chattels alone?
May I not drive a bargain my daughter to "place"?
   Can't I do what I like with my own?

She never upbraids me—I would that she did—
   Her pale face as hopeless as death,
Haunts me morning and night, and will trouble
      me sore,
   Till the hour I inspire my last breath.

As to Fanny, the youngest, I feel so distraught,
   At the troubles revealed to you now,
That if she eloped with the man of her choice,
   I could almost feel happy, I vow.

Nay, pity me not; you have caught me unnerv'd.
   To drive bargains from youth was I trained,
And I knew not things sought by disciples of
      greed,
   Were ashes when grasped and obtained.

For 'tis not in devices invented by man,
   Wealth, title, and glittering show,
That the spirit can rest while sojourning here,
   In mortality cradled below.

It seeks for a love that is dearer than life—
   A pure flame from the realms of the blest;
For a heart which responds to the throbs of its
      own,
   And can hush its complainings to rest.

Like an eagle it rises from fetters of earth,
   And breaking its links to the sod,
Seeks rest in a conscience devoid of reproach,
   And a home at the throne of its God.

WIRBEL-BEWEGUNG.

———

WHAT is Wirbel-bewegung? Who knows anything about Wirbel-bewegung? The secret has
just been extracted that the round world, and
they that dwell therein, the big whales and little
fishes, gorillas and anthropologists, the sun, the
moon, the stars, nay, the foundation of the wide
universe itself, are all Wirbel-bewegung. The
readers of these pages, the writer, the paper, the
printing ink, and the printer's devil, are Wirbel-
bewegung root and branch. Historical person-
ages, Henry VIII., the Holy Maid of Kent, Mr.
Disraeli, the Cock-lane Ghost, Mr. Gladstone,
the Thirsty Woman of Tutbury, the Mayor of
Haverfordwest, the Great Mogul, Landseer's
Lions, and Baalam's Ass, are all nothing more
nor less than Wirbel-bewegung. Who made the

discovery? Professor Sir W. Thomson, of the
Atlantic Cable, who once announced it to an
assemblage of learned philosophers, with Sir
David Brewster at their head, at a crowded
meeting of the members of the Royal Society
of Edinburgh. The present republication of such
an announcement in England is of itself a mighty
task, but now that the first burst is over, and
the secret out, breathing time may be allowed,
and the details calmly considered in fresh para-
graphs. I am now as exhausted as Washing-
ton Irving's hero of old, who took a run of three
miles to jump over a hill, but having reached
the bottom of it, sat down to rest, and then
walked over at his leisure.

All the substances known to exist in the Earth,
the fixed stars, and in meteoric stones, are re-
ducible by the chemist into less than a hundred
simple elements, and many of these are rare.
Indeed it has been computed, with tolerable cer-
tainty, that more than forty-four per cent. of
the solid crust of the Earth is composed of

oxygen, twenty-two per cent. of silicon, nine
per cent. of aluminium, nine of iron, six of
calcium, two of magnesium, two of sodium, and
one of potassium, all other substances being
rarer still. The great bulk of the elementary
bodies are chemical rarities, some of them as
scarce as the metal lithium, which sells at six
shillings a grain, and burns with a magnificent
flame. They are called simple bodies, because
no power at present in the hands of man can
demonstrate them to be composed of two or
more substances. Nevertheless, till recently,
nothing was known of Wirbel-bewegung. A
lump of any solid simple substance is reasonably
assumed to be built up of a number of atoms of
that substance, but such ultimate particles have
never been seen, being infinitely beyond the ken
of the most powerful microscope, so on this point
there is fine scope for the exercise of the imagination. Let a poker, made of the simple
substance iron, be made red hot in the fire,
and it will grow longer than it was when cold;

hence its constituent particles have the power of motion. In fact, heat in a body can be proved to be nothing but motion, and as absolute absence of heat represents a degree of cold that has never been attained on earth—the atoms of all bodies are believed to be in a state of unrest. What that motion is, or what the atoms are like, nobody knows, so it has been assumed, by many philosophers, that the particles are incompressibly hard and infinitely rigid. "But," it has been argued, "it is impossible to imagine an atom so small that it cannot be cut in two, therefore matter may be infinitely divisible." In this case it would not be matter at all, in the ordinary sense of the word. As it is therefore quite as impossible to prove as disprove the existence of solid matter, the dilemma forms a very pretty puzzle; and the leading votaries of physical science at the present day are divided into two classes, the materialists and immaterialists, and the ranks of the latter seem day by day to be gaining ground.

Professor Thomson based his communication upon the admirable discovery of Helmholtz of the law of vortex motion in a perfect fluid, that is to say, in a hypothetical fluid, destitute of viscosity or fluid friction. Helmholtz has proved, mathematically, an absolute unchangeability in the motion of any portion of a perfect fluid in which the peculiar motion he calls "Wirbel-bewegung" has once been created. Professor Thomson, therefore, boldly threw down the gauntlet at Edinburgh, by condemning "the monstrous assumption of infinitely strong and infinitely rigid pieces of matter," and suggested that Helmholtz's rings may be the true atoms. Further, he managed in the presence of the audience, to make some large smoke rings, of the imperfectly elastic fluid, air, and to render them visible to the audience.* These rings floated about the room, and were frequently seen to bound obliquely from one another, shaking vio-

---

* See footnote on page 59.

lently from the effects of the shock. They rebounded from each other, and trembled in much
the same way that two indiarubber belts would
have done under the same circumstances. Had
these rings been formed of a perfect fluid, they
would, as Helmholtz has demonstrated, have
kept up the Wirbel-bewegung motion to all
eternity, and if two such vortex atoms were
interlinked, nothing could ever separate them,
for one line of vortex motion could never pass
through another line; thus such a double vortex
atom might much vary in shape, yet remain
essentially the same.

There are now, at least, four beautiful theories
as to the ultimate constitution of matter. The
first supposes atoms to be solid lumps; the second
imagines them to be forces emanating from points;
the third classes them as Wirbel-bewegung; and
a fourth, propounded by Dr. T. L. Phipson in
the pages of the Parisian *Cosmos*, assumes that
atoms are elastic, thus accounting for the stretching of a poker when it is heated. But why or

how do the atoms stretch? I am going to bring
out a fifth theory some day, when I have time
to find facts to support it, and shall prove that
there are no such things as atoms at all.

So Wirbel-bewegung is vortex motion. In all
ages mysterious powers have been ascribed to
the circle. A serpent with its tail in its mouth
has long been recognised as the fittest emblem
of eternity. Dancing dervishes — devotees of
Wirbel-bewegung—for centuries have achieved a
meritorious amount of devotion by spinning round
upon one leg. The Lamas of Thibet pray by
machinery, their petitions being printed upon
small windmills, which rotate right merrily in
every passing breeze. Sometimes, it is true, the
wind chances to fail, but a band over the smoke-
jack in the chimney furnishes the necessary mechanical power to grind the prayers. The world
is circular, and travels round the sun in a circle;
the moon twists round the earth in a circle;
the sun dances round his axis in a circle, and
is supposed himself to travel in a circle round

the star Alcyone, the centre of another circle;
so there are plenty of precedents for Professor
Thomson's idea that atoms whirl in circles, and
nobody questions that the heads of theorising
philosophers spin round in an endless Wirbel-
bewegung. Astrologers and other clever men
found out the virtues of Wirbel-bewegung long
ago, so made their bodies spin round when performing their incantations. Dr. Aldrovando, first
physician to Prester John, Leech to the Grand
Lama, and Hakim in Ordinary to Mustapha
Muley Bey, is recorded by Ingoldsby to have
thus by unholy rites obtained power over the
spirits of the nether world. " On one side was
an article bearing a strong resemblance to a
coffin; on the other, was a large oval mirror
in an ebony frame; and in the midst of the
floor was described, in red chalk, a double circle
about six feet in diameter; its inner verge
inscribed with sundry hieroglyphics, agreeably
relieved at intervals with an alternation of skulls
and crossbones. In the very centre was deposited

one skull of such surprising size and thickness,
as would have filled the soul of a Spurzheim or
De Ville with astonishment. A large book, a
naked sword, an hour-glass, a chafing dish, and
a black cat, completed the list of moveables.
The Doctor seated himself in the centre of the
circle upon the large skull, elevating his legs
to an angle of forty-five degrees. In this position
he spun round with a velocity to be equalled
only by that of a teetotum, the red roses on his
insteps seeming to describe a circle of fire. The
best buckskins that ever mounted at Melton has
soon yielded to such rotatory friction—but he
spun on—the cat mewed, bats and obscene birds
fluttered overhead." Now, here is a clear case
of Wirbel-bewegung, known to a scientific man
in the days of old. Nowadays, whenever a discovery is made some good natured friend of the
promulgator always rises to say it is not new,
so here is a clear case against Professor Thomson.
Probably he made his discovery by going through
the ceremonial incantations laid down by the

illustrious Dr. Aldrovando, but that is one of the grave secrets his tailor only can unravel. The scientific world travels onwards at a rapid rate, and who knows whether before long the canny folks in Glasgow may not see their learned townsman building himself a house of solid matter, made by banging smoke-rings out of a wooden box with a damp towel.

"POOR OLD JOE!"

[The following lines refer to a somewhat aged Italian who, some years ago, by the aid of two donkeys, carried coals and goods about Haverfordwest, but made existence hideous by his yells whilst performing his useful mission in life. His donkeys were sleek and handsome; he told me that they were his only friends, and that they perfectly understood each other; he illustrated this by asking one donkey to sing, a request with which the animal complied, raising, moreover, his tail, at the moment he uplifted his voice. The other donkey had been taught pantomimic tricks which he would perform at request. Joe was a "character" in his way, and as much a public institution in Haverfordwest as the town clock or the Town Clerk. At the time the following lines were written, Garibaldi and other patriots were engaged in the freeing of Italy.]

Up, up the hilly street,

With wayworn, weary feet,

There they go;

Three of the long-eared race,

One with a human face—

Poor old Joe!

Italia's sunny clime
Hath lost thee for a time:
    Tale of woe!
Whilst her fair freedom grows,
Thou'rt here, a severed rose—
    Poor old Joe!

Thy voice hath lost its tone;
Was it ever sweeter known
    Years ago?
Whate'er it was before,
'Tis like a creaking door—
    Poor old Joe!

Thou'rt upright, all men say,
And true, like poor dog Tray,
    Don't you know?
Who was faithful, true, and kind,
And his tail stuck out behind—
    Poor old Joe!

Well hast thou done thy part,
With honest hand and heart;
And though snow
Thy head may whiten fast,
We'll love thee to the last—
Poor old Joe !

THE HUMAN HIVE.

FROM the mountain's brow
  In the dark cold night,
I view the town
  With its spots of light ;
And the furnace flames
  In the vale below,
Roar up to heaven
  With their fiercest glow,
As men toil on
  At the nod of wealth,
Selling their souls,
  Their peace, their health,
The Dead Sea fruit,
  Striving to clasp—

G

Fair to the sight,
　　Ashes to grasp.

Fitfully, mournfully,
　　On they go,
Sowing the whirlwind,
　　And reaping woe.
Recking nothing
　　But earthly lust,
Heaping up treasure
　　Of golden dust;
Quitting with sorrow
　　Their mother earth,
Grasping the ashes
　　Beloved from birth.
Yet flowers bedeck
　　Each earthly sod,
And the stars of heaven
　　Proclaim a God.

When Mammon lifts
　　His claws of gold,

They serve the god
   With heart a-cold;
And sailing down
   Eternity's flood,
Lay on his altar
   Their lives and blood.
Sad is the tale
   Of the human hive,
Where pain and anguish
   Eternally strive,
For the things of time,
   The dust of earth,
Forgetting alway
   Their spirit birth.

Ere a few short years
   Are gone and sped,
Master and man
   Lie cold and dead.

THE LAY

OF

THE MACE-BEARERS.

———

THREE Sergeants with maces so rich and so rare,
   At Plymouth oft march in advance of the
      Mayor;
When he stops in his walking the Sergeants stop
      too,
   When he smiles they all laugh, when he sighs
      they Boo-hoo.

And some time ago a great British Ass-
   ociation—for plastering science *en masse*
On the back of the nation at large—went to see
   This superior Mayor with his Mace-bearers
      three.

And they marched to the left, and they marched
    to the right,
  As we opened our ranks to their passage that
    night;
Then they swept in a curve round the musical
    band,
  And turned on one leg as they came to a stand.

And we felt that life's glories extend but a span,
  For those maces were made in the days of
    Queen Anne;
And gone are the Mayors who surveyed them of
    old,
  And forgotten their names, like a tale that is
    told.

Their remains in the churchyard rest lowly and
    lone,
  And the ivy creeps over the mouldering stone,
Whose armorial bearings imperfectly tell
  They were linked to the town they befriended
    so well.

When the night-winds of heaven rustle under the
    eaves,
    And the moon casts her sheen on the whisper-
        ing leaves,
By the side of the harbour you often may see
    The ghosts of dead Mayors and their Mace-
        bearers three.

So if you are nervous, or not very well,
    After nine o'clock strikes never leave your hotel;
And from ghosts you'll be safe, it is frequently said,
    If a horse-shoe you nail to the foot of your bed.

You remember, dear reader, how chronicles tell
    Of Admiral Drake, that great nautical swell?
In Plymouth he lived, and when not on the sea,
    Ambled sailor-like after his Mace-bearers three.

Drake's two little eyes, like live cinders ablaze,
    Were set in a forehead resembling red baize;
And his porcupine head in its snowy-white ruff,
    A temper pourtrayed of perpetual huff.

When the Spanish Armada came looming in
 sight,
  Drake was playing at bowls on the eve of the
  fight;
Said he to his Captains—" Let's finish our game;
  We can thrash those land-lubbers in shore just
  the same."

And this fire-eating Mayor, with his lobster-like
 face,
  Oft kicked in the air both the Sergeant and
  mace,
And delighted in hunting *en route* to the sea,
  Those terrified varlets, his Mace-bearers three.

Town-sergeants, in those days, would fly like the
 wind,
  Crying—" Out of the way!   Here's Sir Francis
  behind!"
For Sir Francis loved better than hunting the
 fox,
  The chasing of Mace-bearers into the docks.

But a Mace-bearer now is a man of repute,

    Whose ideas on town government none may
        refute;

His words so precise, and his motions so slow,

    A monarch could not make him quicken —
        Oh, no!

And all nice little boys who in Devonshire dwell,

    Uplift their bright eyes as their grandmammas
        tell

How, if they are good, they hereafter may be

    Of Plymouth the Mayor, and have Mace-bearers
        three.

A LOVE SONG.

———

Away from the noise of cities,
   Away from all man-made things,
Away from the haunts of fashion,
   Away from courts and kings—

We'll wander where nature ruleth,
   Where the glorious sunsets glow,
Where the flowers all diamond-laden
   Unveil their breasts of snow—

Of snow, and violet, and purple—
   Where the birds as free as air,
Shun not our hallowed footsteps,
   Nor dream of death-wiles there.

And there, in the old poke bonnet,
  Whence the wild-flowers deftly swing,
Thine eyes so full of mischief
  Shalt drink the eternal spring

Of a love that knows no meanness,
  Of a love too deep for earth,
Of a love that has pierced the secret
  Of thine unrivalled worth,

Which the world may dim for a season,
  With its bright and glittering shroud—
Oh, hearts are a-cold and aching
  Under the breasts of the proud.

But lightly the chains of fashion,
  And feebly the ties of earth,
Fetter thy noble nature,
  Child of the spirit birth.

There's a love that knows no fading;
  And free from earth's wild unrest,
Its fibres of true affection
  Are rooted within thy breast.

A VISION.

———

Tossing on a bed of fever
    All disquieted I lie,
Visions and strange phantasies
    Flit before my weary eye.
Knarlèd oaks of shady forests
    Throw their arching boughs o'erhead,
And the sunlight streams in patches,
    Whilst the trees their shadows shed
O'er the dense and tangled brushwood,
    O'er the bramble and the thyme,
And the distant bells are ringing
    With a peaceful Sabbath chime.
Lazily the bees are humming
    In the brilliant noontide sheen,

And bright dragon-flies come circling
　　In their mailèd coats of green.
Now a troubled darkness hurtles,
　　And the scene seems streaked with blood;
Now a noise of rushing waters,
　　Of a vast o'erwhelming flood.
A strange unhallowed wind is sighing,
　　And I wake to sense again,
Wake to hear my feeble moaning
　　Tossing on a bed of pain.

Hark! those strains of heavenly music,
　　All unearthly in their tone,
Stealing o'er the troubled senses,
　　Whispering thoughts of realms unknown.
See! the darksome clouds are breaking,
　　Burst by streams of purest light,
And a scene of matchless glory
　　Opens to my dazzled sight.
Terraces of light ascending,
　　Columns, arches, spires, and domes—

Where the pure from earth translated
    Praise Him in their starry homes.
And my long lost sister Edith,
    Beckons with her pale white hand,
She—the loved one—leads me onward,
    Onward to the spirit-land.
Angels of immortal beauty
    Cluster round in robes of light—
Now, ah me! the scene is fading,
    Fading from my longing sight,
And my outstretched hands appealing,
    Plead for entrance there in vain;
And I wake to care and sorrow—
    Wake to misery and pain.

And I press my throbbing temples
    With a sense of awe and dread;
Have I in my fitful slumbers,
    Passed the portals of the dead?
Trod the land of the immortal?
    Pierced the secrets of the tomb?

Scanned the realms of the hereafter,
　　Where the flowers eternal bloom?
If that heaven be so resplendent
　　In the visions of the night,
The reality of glory
　　Is beyond all mortal sight.
And I long to burst my trammels—
　　Seek those regions of the blest,
" Where the wicked cease from troubling
　　And the weary are at rest."

UNDER THE LIMES.

Sitting by the ruined terrace
   In the calm of eventide,
Sadness flings her shadows o'er me,
   Fancy wanders far and wide.
And I hear the winds of autumn
   Whispering sadly through the limes,
Singing, singing, singing ever,
   Of the joys of bygone times.

And my heart is dead within me,
   Cold and frozen as a stone;
Seared by friendship false and lifeless—
   Left to make its bitter moan.

Young in years but not in sorrow,
  Neither blanched by age nor crimes,
Clinging, clinging, clinging ever,
  To the love of bygone times.

And the path where oft we wandered,
  Breathed each living, earnest vow,
And the stars—the trees—the streamlet—
  All, all rise before me now.
And that voice so well remembered,
  E'en again in softness chimes,
Ringing, ringing, ringing ever,
  In the tones of bygone times.

Deep, dark thoughts in sadness linger,
  O'er me cast their gloomy breath—
Tell of one escape from sorrow,
  Through the cypress shades of death;
And the spirit's longings wander,
  While the night-wind shakes the limes.
Winging, winging, winging ever,
  To the scenes of bygone times.

THE ANGEL OF SILENCE.

WITH marble-like feet on the darksome clouds
    Ascending from worlds of woe,
The Angel of Silence in majesty stood,
All patiently calm as the murmuring flood,
Of the passions of men and their deeds of blood,
    Re-echoed from depths below.

And sadly the murmurs of sorrow and pain,
    Of the tide of human tears,
Rose heavenwards with prayers for a time of
    peace,
For the day when the tumult of life should cease,
When the souls of men should obtain release,
    In the march of the silent years.

11

Impassively calm was her snow-white brow,
    As she read the Decrees of Fate,
Whilst down from the blade of her gleaming
    sword,
The radiance of truth in its purity poured,
To those who could grasp the Word of the Lord,
    In the regions of strife and hate.

That Messenger knew that no sign from heaven
    Would to stem the tide avail;
That the web must be woven in human life,
Of the outcome of sin, of the wages of strife,
Till the fruits of repentance with holiness rife,
    Shine forth as the Holy Grail.

The conscience of man must be scarred and stung,
    By the arrows of pain and sin,
By the furnace fires of affliction be tried,
Ere the soul casts away its dark mantle of
    pride,
Not from the power of the voice outside,
    But the might of the thought within.

Hearts by that angel are softened and swayed,
    In the noiseless hours of night;
And in deeds by day is the work outwrought,
For the matchless power of the silent thought,
From realms on high by an Angel brought,
    Floods the wide world with light.

THE

WOBBLEJAW BALLADS.

THE oral traditions of a people live long in the
public memory; they fix in the minds of both young
and old the deeds of heroism of their forefathers;
they set before young people standards which all
admire, and which some few of them, fired by the
spirit of emulation, attempt themselves to reach.
The verses of Congreve, Tennant, and other great
poets of the past, have died out of public memory,
but the legend beginning—

> Please to remember the Fifth of November,
> The gunpowder tree, and the plot —

has been handed down orally from generation to
generation, and with ballad poetry of a more

pretentious character, lives to this day in the hearts
of men.

Why should not the noble deeds of the public
men of our own day be similarly handed down to
posterity? Why should not their acts of heroism
be recorded in flowing verse—in stanzas easily
assimilated by the plastic mind of youth, and which
can readily be set to music, or sung harmoniously
as a Christmas carol?

Folkestone, one of the most attractive seaside
resorts in the beautiful county of Kent, has its
maps and its guide-books, but where do we find any
record of the virtues or of the painstaking labours
of those public men, who have done so much in
their day and generation to raise the town to its
present popularity? Shall bricks and mortar be
remembered in our chronicles, and men of public
worth be forgotten? This must not be.

Thoughts similar to these floated through the
minds of a humble but respectable family, residing
within the limits of the ancient town of Folkestone.
The eldest son, Mr. Anthony Wobblejaws, whose

name is well known throughout the district, resolved, in his homely way, to sing the praises of
the men of public worth whose acts he witnessed
with admiration from a distance, and ambitiously
hoped at some period, however distant, to be in
a position to imitate. His father and mother encouraged him in his efforts, and thus was launched
upon the world a series of ballads, which it is hoped
will send a thrill of admiration for the chief public
men of Folkestone through the dwellers in all lands
upon the face of the earth, and awaken in the
hearts of all readers the kindliest of feelings towards
the gentlemen whose deeds are recorded in the following pages.

THE WOBBLEJAW BALLADS.

No. I.

To the Edditor of the " Folkestone News."

MY DEAR SIR,

My sun Tony have taken to riting poetry, and please print his verses which I send, for he is the clevverest boy in Kent; his own father says so, and I say so too. Mr. Peel, at the Grammer Skule, says he have never seen a skoller like him before, and do not expect to agen.

He is seventeen years old and quite perfect, for me and his father wont let him have any idees but ourn, tho its strange wot notions he picks up for hisself, wich we have to weed out; this gives us a deel of trubble sometimes. He follers the true religion, wich is the Calvanistic Methodist, not of course the Pilgrim Wobblers [Warblers?] branch, wich is wicked and false. We are looking for a wife for him, and have almost decided upon a young woman living in Clifton Gardins; when we have settled in our minds we will let him know. But poor boy, he is young yet; we kept him in petticuts till three years ago, for boys is too fast nowadays, has wicked notions of their own, and makes their parents look old before their time.

Tony says he will rite all about the people in our town, and will put in verse for printing in your papper all the tails anyboddy nose about everyboddy; his verses will be full of fashin and passhin, so them as nose any skandles about someboddy may send them to my son Tony, addressed to the care of the Mare of Folkestone.

Yures truly,

SARAH WOBBLEJAWS.

June 25, 1877.

ON THE APPOINTMENT OF A PUBLIC ANALYST
BY THE CORPORATION OF FOLKESTONE.*

Oh, sound the loud timbrel and bang the big
　　drum,

Let the trumpet peal forth and the double bass
　　hum,

Let soldiers and sailors desist from their pranks

And march to the station with Alderman Banks—

Let men, women, and children in thousands be
　　there,

Shouting "Hip! Hip! Hurrah!"—let our wor-
　　shipful Mayor,

After sounding the gong at the West Cliff Hotel,

Head our march like a King, whilst the Crier,
　　with his bell,

And Captain Charles Cooke with his merry men
　　all,

And Major R. Sigham respond to this call,

---

* A few days before this ballad was written, the Folkestone Town Council appointed Mr. Sydney Harvey, of
Canterbury, as public analyst for Folkestone, he being
considered by far the best candidate for the post.　An
amendment by Mr. Alderman Caister that the question
be deferred, was lost.

The great Sydney Harvey with honours to crown,
As that new public analyst enters the town.

He's a wonderful man! I expect him with dread,
For he always will have his sharp nose in our
bread;
His fingers will dip in our puddings and pies,
Whilst our teas and our sugars will melt in his
eyes
Into sloe leaves, and brickdust, and fine yellow
sand,
Yea, our mustard will change into starch in his
hand.
When our rivers behold him with knowledge so
crammed,
They will ask to be filtered and pray to be
dammed,
And repent having lived with the habits of hogs,
Too fond of foul drains, of "high" cats, and dead
dogs.
He's a wonderful man! A most wonderful man!
Deny it, astute Captain Harpe, if you can.

With tartrate of potash and phosphate of lime,

He'll precipitate Care from the River of Time;

With carbonic anhydride and extract of soap

He will pacify Emperor, Sultan, the Pope,

And Mr. James Jones (who on water is "nuts,"

For in his own house he receives it in butts,

And drinks it in quantities fresh from the wood,

So takes very good care it shall come to him good).

Then shout for S. Harvey! Peal Eanswythe thy
    bells!

Let Envy and Hate shrink in fear to their hells,

Dragging Caister's amendment—that venomous
    snake—

To hot regions below to feed on coke cake.

Shall I tell you, dear friends, how it cometh to
    pass,

That on nitrate of chemiconomenjackass,

Sydney Harvey ascended the Temple of Fame.

And on its best monuments whittled his name?

Ah no! For the story is thrilling and long,

And like Swinburne's verses is racy and strong,

Full of love and devotion, and slaughter and
    pelf—
(The fact is I know naught about it myself,
So will gently back out with politeness and grace,
On the plea of regard for your diamond-like space),
So " Long live the Queen ! " and "Three cheers for
    the Mayor ! "
When you see us together you'll own we're a
    pair.

ANTHONY WOBBLEJAWS.

THE WOBBLEJAW BALLADS.

No. II.

To the Edditor of the " Folkestone News."

DEAR MR. EDDITOR,

I have very important things to tell you abbout, and dont know where to begin. To cut my tail short, the day after you printed Tony's verses, a member of the Copperashun nocked at our door; he had a red rose in his button-hole, a blue weskit, and a new white hat, just like a prince.

" Fine mornin', Mrs. Wobblejaws," sez he.

" The same to you, sir," sez I, "and thank you kindly."

" Mr. Anthony's a clever young man," sez he; "but," sez he, wheedling-like, "don't you think he's a leetle—jist a verry leetle—bit personal in his verses?"

" Not a bit of it," sez I, quite prompt.

"I won't presoom to contradict you," sez he, smilin' feebly, and rubbin' his hands, and lookin' half fritened, "for a lady of your experience must know best," sez he, quite nice; "but ask him pleese, to say less about me, and more about Pledge and the other fellers," sez he.

"I'll consider about it, sir," sez I, quite grand.

Then he seezed little Betsy Perry, as was playing on the steps, and kissed her agen and agen.

"A finer, blesseder, prettier girl than this o' yours, I never see," sed he, "she's so like her mother, I should know her anywheres."

"She aint mine," I replide, "she's the brat o' Nancy Perry, wich I hates."

He turns red, and sets her down sharp agen the new painted green railins, and sez—

"Dear me, how shortsited I'm gettin', Mrs. Wobblejaws," and off ran the child skreeming like a green gridiron.

I send you some more of Tony's verses, all about Giniral Grant leaving England. I wish you had

seen me and the Town Clerk at his welcum that
day.—Yures truly,

SARAH WOBBLEJAWS.

————

THE DELIVERY OF AN ADDRESS TO GENERAL GRANT BY THE CORPORATION OF FOLKESTONE, JULY 5th, 1877.

With flags and with banners all Folkestone looked
gay,
And boys cleared their windpipes and shouted
" Hooray ! "
Whilst the station was filled with a glittering
throng,
To welcome the hero, the theme of my song.

Oh firm was the step of bold General Grant,
With his hat, as the Yankees say, "full on the
slant ;"
" Yankee Doodle " he whistled while marching
along,
Did this greatest of heroes, so stout and so
strong.

The Mayor in his robes looked most scrumptiously
    fine,
And his Aldermen three were drawn up in a line—
Messrs. Hoad, Banks, and Caister, were all of
    them there,
And the Town Sergeant also to wait on the Mayor.

All lively as grasshoppers fresh from the Lees,
They said to the General—" Sir, if you please,
Our Clerk will now read you a friendly address—"
" Si-lence!" roared the Sergeant, on "*Si*" putting
    stress.

" With very great pleasure," the General said,
" Will I hear that 'ere dockyment properly read;
But the steamer's a-waiting, so pray, sirs, be quick:"
And he sat ·down good-humouredly whittling a
    stick.

Then the Mayor and the Aldermen opened the roll,
Which the Clerk read aloud with much feeling and
    soul,

Until tears began flowing from every eye,

And his pathos elicited many a sigh.

> " We, the Worshipful the Mayor,
>   We, the Aldermen and Burgesses
> Of most ancient Folkestone's town,
>   Deeply and sincerely urgesses
> Your striking individual merit,
>   Your undisputed capabilities ;
> So welcome you on this here pier,
>   Which at the bottom of the hill it is."

Here the Clerk paused for breath, and benignly

   looked round,

Whilst from those within earshot there came not a

   sound,

Then beginning again the Clerk waved his hand,

And continued in accents impressive and grand—

> " Our two all-fired important nations,
>   Please give us aid in well cementing ;
> But just remember, Mister Grant,
>   This land of freedom never went in
> For living mermaids made by Barnum,
>   Wooden nutmegs, brandy cocktails,
> Woolly horses, and those marvels
>   Which of Yankees form the stock tales."

Here a chuckle and giggle from Alderman Banks

Made the Mayor look severe at a man on his flanks,

Till he saw the real culprit was one of his clan,

When he smiled, though he wished him at far
   Teheran.

> " We hope your son will grow in wisdom,
>   Will imitate his worthy father,
> Will whip creation with his cuteness,
>   And outshine you, sir—don't we rather !
>   Given under our Corporate Seal,
>   (With wax from Riley's) in the Town Hall,
>   *Signed :*—A. Wobblejaws, J. Sherwood,
>   And W. Harrison, to crown all."

Then said General Grant with the sweetest of
   smiles—

" I have travelled, my friends, some few thousands
   of miles,

But never expected a welcome like this ;

I feel, 'pon my soul, in the regions of bliss.

" When nations like ours are conjoined hand in
   hand,

Our strength so united no power can withstand ;

We can trample out wars, bid disturbances cease,

And establish afar the pure empire of peace.

" Your municipal government seemeth to me

A very strong branch in your liberty's tree,

So, Hurrah! ye brave Britons, who ne'er will be
    slaves !

And who live on roast beef from your birth to
    your graves.

" And now Mr. Mayor, I must bid you farewell,

With gratitude greater than mortal can tell;

And to you Mr. Hoad, also you Mr. Banks,

Mr. Caister likewise, do I tender my thanks."

Then cheers from the people, and tunes from the
    band,

Reached the steamship " Victoria " far from the
    land ;

And Sir Edward Watkin atop of the pier,

Cried " Ochone! he is leaving us! Bless me! oh
    dear ! "

ANTHONY WOBBLEJAWS.

THE WOBBLEJAW BALLADS.

No. III.

To the Edditor of the "Folkestone News."

Mr. Edditor,

Did you know that jeenyus cums down from father to sun?

Tony sez that other things cum down in the same way, and that our minds stamp their marks upon our boddies, and the minds and boddies of them that cum after us.   He sez, sum yung peeple have diseeses and deformitys, cos of the lies their parrents told in trade and elseware.

Here's wot Tony's father rit and printed sum yeers ago.

Truly yures,

SARAH WOBBLEJAW.

THE RIFLE CORPS.

Mr. Edditor—Sir,—Our invinsible rifles,
Who fight like cock bantams, and stick not at
    trifles,
Came over this way, sir, a few days ago,
A marchin' like fiddlers, sir, all of a row.
Then the noise that they made, it was awful! O
    dear!
All the farmer fokes rownd was a dyin' with fear.
Of the frite which they caused, the akkount which
    I send,
Was written in Lundun, dear sir, by a frend.
I have no more to say, and no longer will trubble
    you,
And am yures very truly,

                 Theophilus W.

———

"Whoi, Joe, my lad, who be these men,
    All dressed so 'nation grand?
For zartin 'tis as voine a sight
    As any in the land.

I've locked my Zairey up, d'ye see,
    Else arter 'em she'd run,
For when she sees red coats she's off,
    Just loike a loaded gun."

" Whoi lawks," said Joe, "and doan't 'ee know?
    They're Veather-beds from town,
With their Capten marchin' at their head—
    Him with the whiskers brown.
They're going to the park to vight,
    And kill each other there,
Though now they look so vriendly too—
    'Tis true, I do declaro!
And those who're left will zack the place,
    And carry off our woives,
And take away our virniture,
    And maybe end our loives!"

" Well, Joe lad, this be zorry news,
    We must defend our homes,
And try and give them roiful chaps
    A toaste of broaken boans;

Zo we will drop in at the " Bull,"

And lest our pluck should vail,

We'll keep it up with many a sup

Of brother Joiles's ya-ale." *

---

* These three verses were written by a friend of the
author of "The Lazy Lays."

THE WOBBLEJAW BALLADS.

No. IV.

To the Edditor of the "Folkestone News."

Mr. Edditor,

The plot is a thikkening. Mr. James Jones
have brought me, and the ballads, and Tony,
publikly under the notis of the Mare and copperashun in conclave, at their last meetin, and every
face was pale at the gravity of the okkashun, and
to-day I see our Town Crier a sittin on his door
step, and pollishin up of his bell with a bit of
lether and a old gluv.

"O," ses he, "Mrs. Wobblejaws, marm, you've
caught me."

"Which?" ses I, as grand as the Empress of
Inja, for aint I Tony's mother?

"Well," he replide, "Jones have introdoosed
you and yure most exlent sun—tell him I sed
'exlent'—to our Counsle and Copperashun, which
meens warm work for all publik servents, for all

them as feel the cares of pomp and state," ses he, sighin; "so I've bought a noo umbrella and a noo pare of shoes, and now I'm a pollishin up of my bell with brickdust from Spinks's," ses he.

"Wornt Jones wild?" ses I, larfin, "but he's a good man, is Jones; he's one as is respektid by me, and the Town Clerk, and Tony, and all Folkestone."

"I shood think he is," sed the Crier. "Why," sed he, starin thru a cloud as was in the sky, and with a solem fur-away look as if he cood see the end of evverything, "I've knowd Jones, on and off, man and boy, sixty-seven years cum next Mikklemuss, and there aint nobody, ne'er a one on em, as can say *that* agen him," ses he, a snappin of his fingers, and stretching out one leg, and aksdently upsettin a little boy with milk cans.

"Verry tru, verry tru," ses I, pikkin up the little boy wrong end uppermost in the excitement of my feelings. *"Adoo! Or revawr!"* sed the Town Crier, and we parted.

Wats to be dun with my sun Tony? He have

fallen in luv with Rose Tomkinson, as is the art-fullest creetur in Folkestone. O, she's deep, she is. She gits people to like her, by nevver sayin nothing aggenst noboddy; she nevver jines in our little talks abbout our nabers, or helps to put down them as oght to be put down. Tony's sister trys to pick quarrels with her, and I'm skarsely sivvle to her when Tony's out of the room. Ugh! The apricot!

"Tony," ses I, "yure a disgrasing of us; me and yure father intended you for Sophy Wilkins, as would make us the best people in our chapple, and would drive the Whiffens so ravin jellus that they would nevver sit easy agen at prares in their pue on Sundays, and wood nevver forgive us to their dyin day."

"Tony," ses his sister, burstin out cryin, "you'll be the ruin of us all, and I shant get engaged as lady's made to the rectoress thru the influens of Sophy Wilkins."

Heer Tony's little bruther, who didnt understan wot was said, begun to cry too.

"Tony," sed Miss Spriggs, his aunt, "I think all luv makkin is wikked and sinfle, and yure parents is too good to you in lettin you think even of Sophy Wilkins. Ware do you expect to go to when you die?"

"Tony," ses his father, "I'm greeved, deeply greeved. Yure a proddigle sun, sir; yure a flying in the face of provvidence, and bringin of the gray hares of yure parents in sorrer to the grave.——"

"Stop there," I sed, "I havvent got eny gray hares."

"Considerin," ses he—not heedin—"considerin the influens of deacon Erasmus Wilkins in our chapple, considerin the aid he mite hev been to me in bisniss, I look upon you as a proffligit, and hope you'll read all about Annienias and Saffira before you go to bed to-nite, and that yure heart will be sofened. I would have you think," ses he, wavin his hand ellerquent, "I would have you think of the futur of them disobedyent children as is predestined to perdishun. Befor we

go to bed to-nite we will all sing the improving
hym :—

> 'Mid seas of never-ending flames,
> Where vengeance dire in thunder rolls,
> And darts to inflict immortal pains,
> Poison the blood of damnèd souls."

Heer I cried with joy, and thot I was in hevven.
Our minnister nevver spuk better than did Tony's
father that nite.

"I have nevver had so much trubble," ses he,
"since the day them three twins come; the other
two of em never disgrased me, but _you_ Tony——"
here he berried his eyes in his hankerchef.

Then Tony got up, verry red, and sed, "I dont
want to be misrespectful, father, but I bleeve
yure all carin more abbout yurselves than about
me, an I think more peeple is married by their
familys than of there own akkord."

"Well, and what would bekum of the Divorse
Court, and your Unkel John's bisness as a lawyer,
if it wasn't so?" ses I.

"Anyhow," replide Tony, "I dont like this
byin and sellin of human creeturs, and I think

its despritly wikked for awl father and you say, and I hope Miss Wilkins will be at the bottom of the well in Seagate Street, before Harvey annelieses it again." And he went out.

Heer's trubble! Heer's trubble!

And now, Mr. Edditor, there's a look in his eye as I dont like, and my mind misgives me that he wont give in. He has all his mothers determinashun, but in him its obstinisy, for he wont give in when he's rong, and I never give in, because I'm always rite, and thats the differens between us. I'm sorry he have not dun enny verses for you this week about the luvly skanddles that hev bin brought to him, but next week let them as thinks their private affares isnt known to noboddy look out.

Yures in trubble,

SARAH WOBBLEJAWS.

TONY'S LAMENT.

DEAR SIR,

My mother has sent you nothing from me this week. There have been troubles in our house too sacred for the public ear, so I cannot let you know the subject or any of the particulars. Perhaps, however, the few lines which follow may be acceptable :—

As the Earth with its maddened cargo
On the path of the ages rolls,
And cries of sorrow and anguish
Pour sadly from human souls,
One wonders why it was created,
'Neath the shade of a mystical ban,
Why the Councils of God and the angels
Should result in the making of man.
But vain are the throbbings of sorrow,
And vain is the weakness of tears,
When man should be up and be doing
Dismayed not by shadowy fears.

So as soon as this fit has passed over,
And joy has abolished "the blues,"
Your Tony, as faithful as ever,
Will send some more lines to the *News*.

ANTHONY WOBBLEJAWS.

THE WOBBLEJAW BALLADS.

No. V.

To the Edditor of the " Folkestone News."

DEAR SIR,

Tony sez he is miserable at home ; he goes about on the hills, stickin' beetles, flise, and sichlike, with pins. He takes them to Mr. Fitzgerald at the Museum ; he is a grate frend of Tony's, and always speeks well of him.

Tony is keeping July Bugs shut up in a glass hive for to studdy them. Tony's father likes this experriment ; he sez that, now there in a hive, p'raps they will lern to make hunny, and be more proffitible than bees, because there bigger, and we shall all make our fortunes.

I send you his last verses.

Truly yures,

SARAH WOBBLEJAWS.

K

THE JULY BUG.

On yester eve I trod the hills
　　Above the Dover Road,
While sunset tinted hill and sea,
　　And fast the tide outflowed.

But darkness hurtled in the air,
　　A cloud approached amain ;
It was not fog, it was not smoke,
　　And much too low for rain.

And nearer, nearer still it came,
　　Brown as my railway rug ;
" Can, can it be ?" I wildly said—
　　" Yes ! 'Tis the July Bug."

As big as beetles were the things,
　　They gave a nasty hum,
They whirled in myriads round my head,
　　" Yet still," said I, " they come."

They crawled adown my graceful neck,
　　They twisted in my hair,
Ran up my sleeve, crawled down my boots,
　　But found no solace there.

One crashed against my Grecian nose,
　　And fell with sullen roar ;
Another fat one on my lips
　　Would fain my mouth explore.

A July Bug in evening flight,
　　Nor reason shows nor rule ;
He knocks his head 'gainst every post—
　　In short he is a fool ;

So I dislike the July Bug,
　　Just as the women state
They do not mind an ugly man,
　　But a born fool they hate.

Last night in dreams I saw a Bug
　　With mailèd head-gear crowned,
I'm sure he measured eight feet long,
　　And nearly seven feet round.

And in the doorway he reclined
    Of Mr. Goodliffe's shop;
He jumped and shouted from behind,
    And pushed him with a mop.

The Crier stood by his right ear,
    Making a hideous din ;
His biggest bell he jerked with force,
    And drove the music in,

Whilst Mr. Wilshere and two men
    Pulled at his third left leg ;
He troubled not—that stolid Bug—
    "It's all in vain," he said.

Some handcuffs Mr. Wilshere then
    Produced amid much chaff;
Even the blockhead of a Bug
    Could not forbear a laugh.

Flat irons lent by Mr Poole
    Were next thrown at the Bug,
And somewhat marred his calm repose;
    They made him shake and shrug.

Said Mr. Poole—" I witnessed how
  He twisted, as he fell,
The chimney-pot askew upon
  The *Rendezvous* Hotel."*

" Oh ! That explains it !" Hogben said,
  " I heard a curious creak,
And thought rheumatic Moggs's knees
  Were extra bad this week."

They from the Harbour Station fetched
  An old horse full of game,
Who " makes up" trains when left alone,
  And " Jemmy" is his name.

A rope was tied around the necks
  Of Jemmy and the Bug,
And crowds in High Street watched them pass,
  With many a pull and tug.

---

* An examination of the chimney-pot will prove to
anybody the truth of my vision.—A. W.

Near Griffith's shop they strained the rope
  And nearly broke their necks,
Because the Bug *would* stop to read
  The bill about blank cheques.

At last within a slight machine,
  For bathing on the beach,
The Bug was caged by Jemmy's aid,
  So go not, I beseech

You, into that machine to-day,
  But listen at the door,
And if the Bug is in it still,
  You'll hear his gentle snore.

Hark ! Do you hear the Boulogne boat ?
  Or is it yonder tug ?
Is it a talking telephone ?
  No.   'Tis the July Bug.

Long live the Queen ! Long live the Mayor !
  Long live Spearpoint also,
And when another Bug is trapped
  Be sure I'll let you know.

                              ANTHONY WOBBLEJAWS.

THE WOBBLEJAW BALLADS.

No. VI.

To the Edditor of the "Folkestone News."

DEAR SIR,

TONY is bringing his ballads to a close for the present. Everyboddy wants to know what he will rite about when he takes up his pen again. He has plenty of subjiks in hand, as follers:—How a milingtery ossifer fired at a targit, and hit a heel-pie man in Sandgate. How Alderman Caister seed a ghost. What the stashun master sed to his men, and what the men sed to the stashun master. Miss Rosylinder Smith and the curate. The luvs of the Mares of Folkestone, which Tony ses is an anshent and ossifide subjik. Alderman Banks on the pollushun of rivers. How a sharp blade and a speer point, was found in the mail bags contriry to regulations. We want more skandles, and let them as nose them, rite all abbout them to the Mare, for Tony, but good bye to all frends for a time.

Truly yures,

SARAH WOBBLEJAWS.

THE CONVERTED CARMAN.

DEAR SIR,

AT the Wesleyan Home Mission meeting last week, under the presidency of Mr. Fagg, the Rev. W. D. Walters made a statement, which I took down at the time, that a workman in Mr. Spurgeon's flock was suddenly moved to speak to a carman in the street about his soul; the man swore at him, but finally was induced to go to the Tabernacle, which he afterwards said he would never enter again. The next time the carman saw Mr. Spurgeon's follower in the

street he took to his heels, but was pursued,
caught, induced to go to the Tabernacle again,
and was, with his wife, converted, and is now
a useful member of the church. I have filled
in the details of this story from imagination,
thus:—

In one of Folkestone's chapels,
   On the fifth day of July,
Eighteen-hundred-and-seventy-seven,
   With mouth agape sat I.

And Mister Walters told his tale,
   Whilst deacons all-a-row,
In nicely studied attitudes,
   Smiled on their flock below.

The preacher's hair was curly black,
   His face was rosy red,
And rosier, ruddier still it grew,
   As thus he sung or said:—

"In the bright sun on London Bridge
 A pale-faced workman stood,
Who groaned, and upwards rolled his eyes,
 He was so very good.

"And that same bilious carpenter
 A carman rude espied,
Who cracked his whip and cried, 'Ya-hip!'
 So after him he hied.

"His shiny cap had one great peak
 Just half-way down his back,
And for an apron this pure child
 Of nature wore a sack.

"His trowsers, made of corduroy,
 Were tied below the knee,
As is the custom of his class,
 Most beautiful to see.

"His blouse of canvas fluttered free,
 He bore his heavy whip
Beneath his arm, did this rude man—
 The man who yelled 'Ya-hip!'

"Now, had that man read Coleridge
    He would have cried, d'ye see,
  'I prithee, ancient carpenter,
    Now wherefore stopp'st thou me?'

"But, 'You get out!' was all he said,
    And snapped amain his whip,
Then set his legs a-swing again,
    And once more cried, 'Ya-hip!'

"'Oh, go not thus!' said Spurgeon's child,
    'But listen unto me,
Here is a ticket, blue and red,
    For our next weekly tea.'

"'Your tea be blowed,' said that rough man,
    With look of strange surprise,
And added sundry bad remarks
    About his limbs and eyes.

"'I will not let thee say me nay,'
    The carpenter replied;
Then both his eyes that carman rubbed,
    And opened very wide.

" For had the stranger punched his head,
    Or sworn an oath or two,
  The carman would have been at home,
    Nor puzzled what to do.

" So lest his brains should be fatigued
    In solving this hard knot,
  He took the ticket, went to tea,
    And found it strong and hot.

" And deaconesses spoke him fair,
    And so did Spurgeon too;
  They were so very nice all round,
    He felt in quite a stew.

" That night he passed in fitful dreams,
    Brought on by hymns and tea;
  His simple brains were so upset,
    All in a whirl was he.

" When next he saw the carpenter
    Close by his waggon's wheels,
  That sturdy carman dropped his whip,
    And took unto his heels.

" But the good carpenter gave chase,
    Joined by a crowd of boys,
  And once more into thraldom led
    The man in corduroys.

" He brought him back to Spurgeon's flock,
    And with him came his wife;
  And that bluff man reformed his ways,
    And led a better life.

" In the great Tabernacle's hall
    They oft stand side by side—
  The carpenter and carman both—
    To Spurgeon's joy and pride.

" And oft he tells his listening flock
    How censures leave a smart,
  But kind words go like arrows home
    To every human heart."

  The moral Walters drew from this,
    All in a nutshell lies—
" *You can reclaim your brother man,*
    So go and do likewise."

Some tea-tickets I straightway bought,
    And though Spearpoint * may rail,
To-night I'll stop and clean convert
    The man who drives the mail.

                    ANTHONY WOBBLEJAWS.

---

* The Folkestone Postmaster.

THE END.

www.ingramcontent.com/pod-product-compliance
Lightning Source LLC
Chambersburg PA
CBHW021122020726
47500CB00003B/873